RIDE THE COLD WIND

Paco, a little Peruvian Indian shepherd, sat watching over his flock of llamas. Below him he could see the cold, blue water of Lake Titicaca sparkling under the hot sun. He could see his own adobe village beside the lake. Far away, Paco saw the giant peaks of the Andes Mountains, covered with snow.

"How dull it is here," Paco sighed, and thought of his father fishing on the lake with the other men of the village. How he longed to be a fisherman, too, and ride the cold wind in a swift reed boat instead of tending the stubborn, disobedient llamas. Then, too, there was a mysterious great fish to be caught—the one the village folk called *El Rayo de Oro*, Golden Lightning. But that time was far off, for there was great danger out on the lake and fishing was man's work.

But at last the lure of the lake was too strong. One early morning, Paco and his sister Pepita took the boat out alone onto the blue, dark waters of Lake Titicaca. And it was there that Paco came up against his dream in an unexpected manner.

Also by Anico Surany and Leonard Everett Fisher:
THE GOLDEN FROG

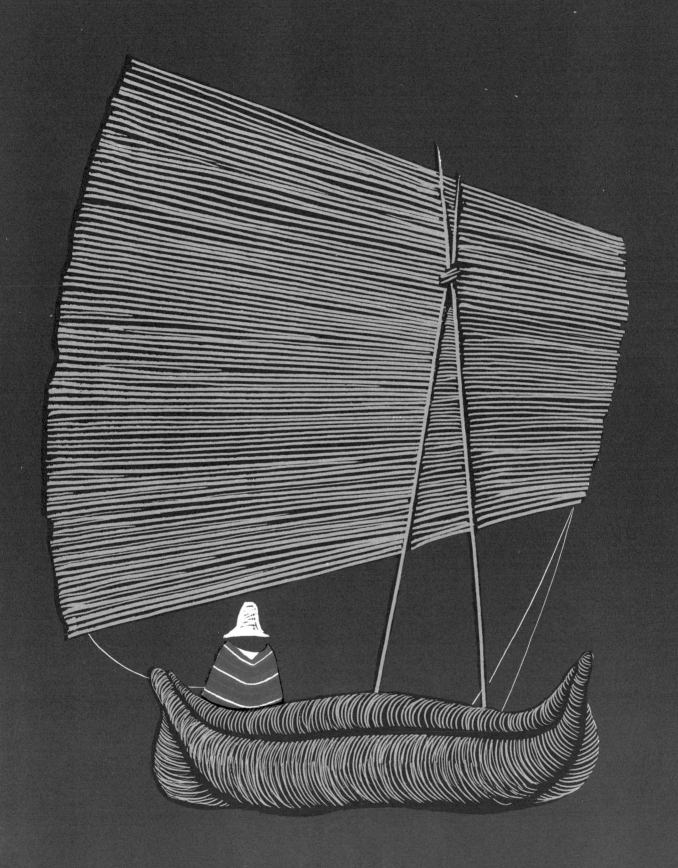

Ride
the Cold Wind

story by Anico Surany

pictures by Leonard Everett Fisher

G. P. Putnam's Sons • New York

For Ildico

Sixth Impression

Text © 1964 by Anico Surany
Illustrations © 1964 by Leonard Everett Fisher
Library of Congress Catalog Card Number: 64-18038
   All rights reserved
Manufactured in the United States of America
Published simultaneously in the Dominion of
   Canada by Longmans Canada Limited, Toronto
07210

RIDE THE COLD WIND

A flock of llamas were nibbling the green grass which grew between the brown boulders. As they scampered among the rocks, the tinkling of their collar bells echoed sharply in the thin highland air.

Paco, a little Peruvian Indian shepherd, sat watching over his dancing flock.

Below him, Paco could see the cold, blue water of Lake Titicaca sparkling under the hot sun. He could see his own adobe village beside the lake. Far away, Paco saw the giant peaks of the Andes Mountains covered with snow.

When the llamas strayed too far, Paco would call them back with a whistle or hissing sounds. But sometimes the proud animals paid no heed to Paco's orders. The stubborn llamas did as they pleased.

"Come back," Paco shouted as he chased after them. "Come back, you silly pests." Stopping for a moment, the haughty llamas would stare at the little shepherd. They would patiently wait until Paco had almost caught up to them. Then the llamas would scatter in all directions over the hillside. And the ornery animals had to be brought back one by one.

"I mustn't lose any of them," Paco grumbled. For the useful llamas carried to market the barley and potatoes which his mother grew behind their house.

As he clambered over the jagged rocks, Paco could see the rush sails of the fishermen's *balsas* on the lake. The reed boats were pushed across the water by the singing winds of the mountains. His own father, Alvaro, was fishing there on the lake.

"How dull it is here," Paco sighed. "Nothing ever happens! How I wish I could be with Father on the *balsa*, riding the cold wind. I'm tired of taking care of these pesky, rude llamas.

"Ay, to be able to catch the great golden fish, the one that hides at the bottom of the lake," Paco thought.

All the people in his village knew about the biggest rainbow trout, which they had named *El Rayo de Oro*, Golden Lightning. Although many of the village fishermen had seen him, not one had managed to catch him.

In the evening, Paco would sadly take his flock home. His sister, Pepita, would skip to the edge of the village to meet him. Hand in hand they would walk home together.

Night after night while eating his dinner before the smoky fire, Paco would ask his father the same question. "When can I go fishing with you, Papa?" he said. "Pepita is old enough to tend our llamas. I'm big enough now to go fishing with you."

"No, *hijo*, you're still too small to handle a net or fishing line," Alvaro replied. "You'll have to wait until you are bigger and stronger. Oh, I know that I've taken you and Pepita sailing in the *balsa* many times. But there is great danger out on the lake, and fishing the whole day is man's work."

Paco's father and mother shook their heads wearily. They were tired of listening to his endless pleading.

"But I *am* strong," Paco thought. "Wait! I'll show Papa how I can handle a fishing line and the boat. How can I make Father understand how I long to be out on the lake riding the cold wind?" Paco had tried to explain so many times. Only Pepita knew how much it meant to him.

That night before falling asleep beside Pepita, Paco whispered excitedly to her. "Pepita, I've a wonderful plan! But you must help me."

Then they spoke softly together in the dark for a few minutes. On hearing his plan, Pepita said, "*Si*, Paco. *Si*, I'll help you!" Closing his eyes, Paco dreamt that he was in the *balsa* fishing, and *El Rayo de Oro* was fighting and jumping at the end of his line.

The next morning long before their parents were up, Paco gently poked Pepita. "Psst, it's time, let's go," he said.

They tiptoed out of the house. In the frosty dawn, they quietly crept to the lake's edge where their father's *balsa* was tied. After pushing it out on the icy water, Paco and Pepita jumped into the boat. Pink flamingos and ducks, startled by the noise, whirred up out of the reeds which grew in the shallows.

Paco unfurled the rush sail. The cold wind blew the boat across the water like a cork. The brisk morning air made their faces tingle. Paco and Pepita laughed happily. They were alone in the *balsa* — out on the great lake!

Paco could see the other village fishermen in their boats throwing their lines into the blue lake. They scooped the gleaming fish from the water with their nets.

Paco fished while Pepita held the sail. Before long, a small pile of little silver fish lay at their feet. Paco was so busy that he hardly noticed how tired his arms were or how his back ached. Nor did he see the black storm clouds moving from the mountains to the lake.

The water became choppy and the cold wind blew stronger. It took all Pepita's strength to hold the sail steady as it flapped in the wind.

Paco cast his line into the foamy water. Suddenly, he felt a great tug at the end of his line. He pulled with all his might! After working and tugging for a long time, he saw a huge, wavy shadow in the water.

"*El Rayo de Oro!* I've caught *El Rayo de Oro!*" Paco shouted to Pepita.

As he fought the great trout, the fishing line cut deeply into his hands. No matter how hard Paco pulled, *El Rayo* would leap high into the air. Then he would flash away in a shower of spray. Paco's hands hurt so much that he could barely hold the line.

"Pepita, Pepita, help me, help me!" Paco cried. "He's getting away, I can't hold him."

"Ay, Paco," his frightened sister called back as the *balsa* rocked back and forth, "I can't help you. I must hold the sail. Let the fish go!"

"No, no," Paco screamed, "I'll catch him." And then, *splash!* Paco fell into the icy lake. The line tore from his hands. *El Rayo* vanished in the deep water.

Sputtering and coughing, Paco began to sink into the black depths. Just as the water covered his face, he felt a pair of strong arms lifting him up. He looked up and saw his father's stern face.

"Ay, foolish little ones, we found you just in time," Alvaro said. "When I found you and the *balsa* missing, I knew where you were. Our neighbor and I quickly came out to get you."

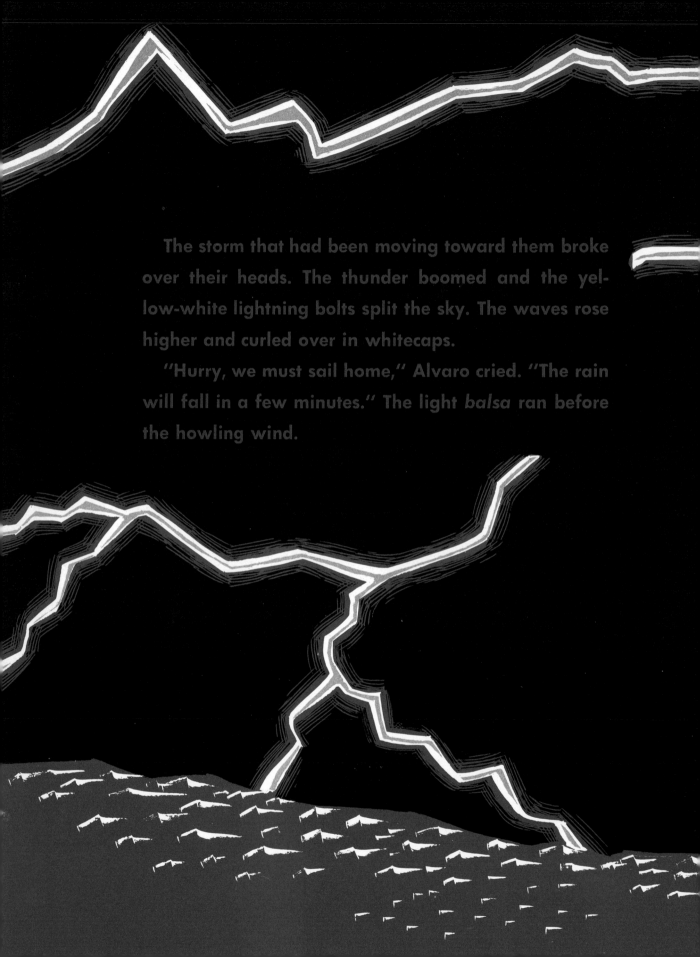

The storm that had been moving toward them broke over their heads. The thunder boomed and the yellow-white lightning bolts split the sky. The waves rose higher and curled over in whitecaps.

"Hurry, we must sail home," Alvaro cried. "The rain will fall in a few minutes." The light *balsa* ran before the howling wind.

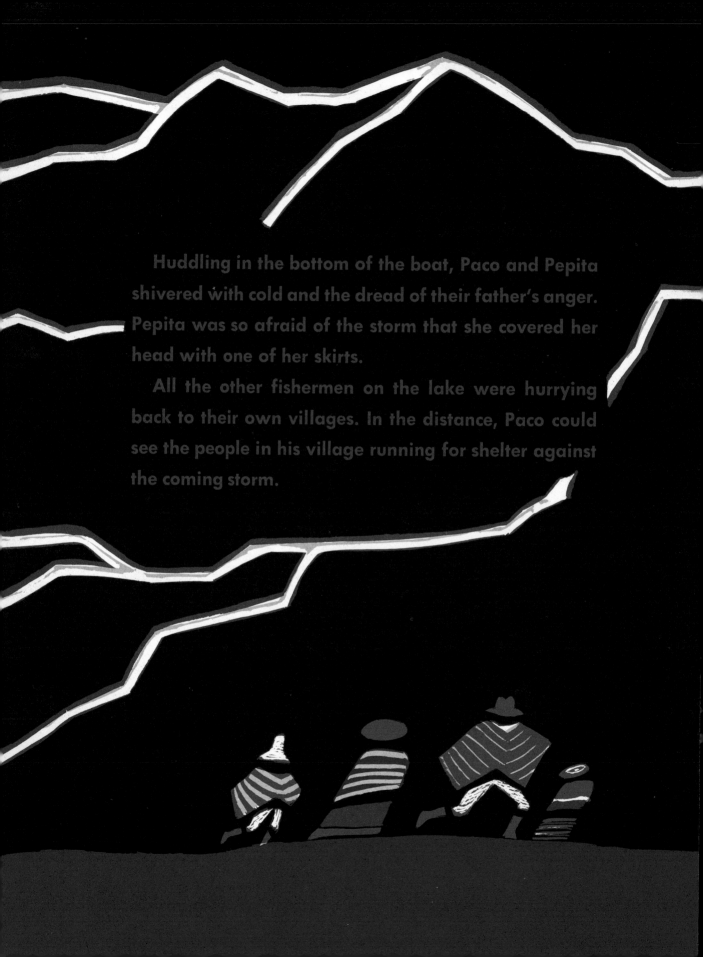

Huddling in the bottom of the boat, Paco and Pepita shivered with cold and the dread of their father's anger. Pepita was so afraid of the storm that she covered her head with one of her skirts.

All the other fishermen on the lake were hurrying back to their own villages. In the distance, Paco could see the people in his village running for shelter against the coming storm.

As the *balsa* glided to shore, Paco and Pepita could see their mother waiting anxiously for them. "You've brought them back safely," she said gratefully to Alvaro. "I was so worried!"

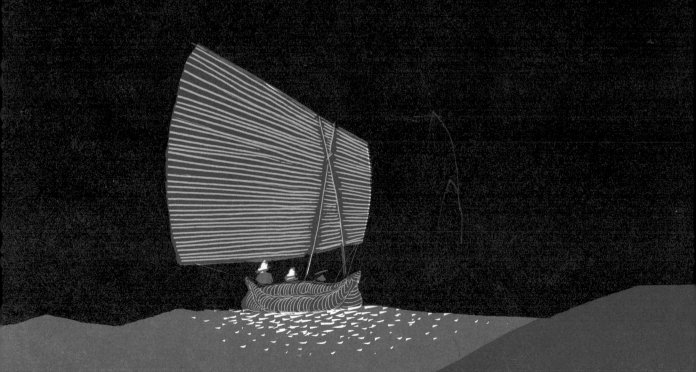

Alvaro carried the children into the house. "Here they are," he said severely, "our brave fisherman and his helper. They should be punished!" Then Alvaro smiled and said, "But I think the lake has punished them for us."

Paco and Pepita were so glad to be home. They sat wrapped in a blanket before the warm fire. Paco now knew that fishing on the lake was man's work. He would have to wait until he was bigger and stronger before he could become a fisherman like his father.

The next day, when Paco was watching over the llamas, he didn't say, "How dull it is here." Nor did he mind chasing after the llamas. For Paco understood that when the right time came, he too would be a fisherman and ride the cold wind. *El Rayo de Oro* was at the bottom of Lake Titicaca waiting to be caught. Then, if Paco hooked him, the great golden trout would never get away!

The Author

Readers who enjoyed *The Golden Frog* will recognize the colorful style of Anico Surany in this new tale of Latin America. Anico Surany was born in Paris, but moved to El Salvador and later Panama when she was a child. Now living with her husband in New York, she is engaged in full-time writing, but still makes trips to Central and South America as often as the occasion permits. *Ride the Cold Wind*, like its predecessor, is the result of the author's deep interest in Latin America.

The Artist

Leonard Everett Fisher, a painter, author and former dean of a professional art school, is the illustrator of more than 75 books for young people. A native New Yorker, Mr. Fisher was graduated from Yale University's School of Fine Art where he was awarded the Weir Prize and Winchester Fellowship. In 1950 he became the thirty-third recipient of the Pulitzer Art Prize. In recent years Mr. Fisher has turned his attention to the illustration and design of children's books and educational materials. He has taken part in various academic conferences and seminars on the art of children's books. He, his wife and their three children make their home in Westport, Connecticut.